JE
R

Rockwell
My nursery school

pre-3

MY NURSERY SCHOOL

Harlow Rockwell

Greenwillow Books

A Division of William Morrow & Company, Inc., New York

For Mrs. Shockley

1 2 3 4 5 80 79 78 77 76

Library of Congress Cataloging in Publication Data
Rockwell, Harlow. My nursery school. Summary: A child discusses the various
activities going on in nursery school.   1. Nursery schools—Juvenile literature.
[1. Nursery schools]   I.   Title.   LB1140.2.R62   372.21'6   75-25871
ISBN 0-688-80025-4   ISBN 0-688-84025-6 lib. bdg.

I go to nursery school.

There are two teachers

and ten children in my room.

There are six guppies in a tank

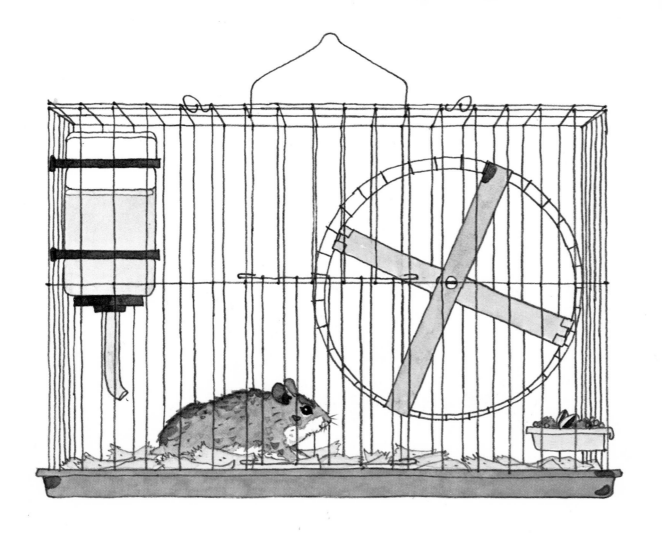

and a furry hamster in a cage.

This is the seed that I am growing.

The little one is Andy's.

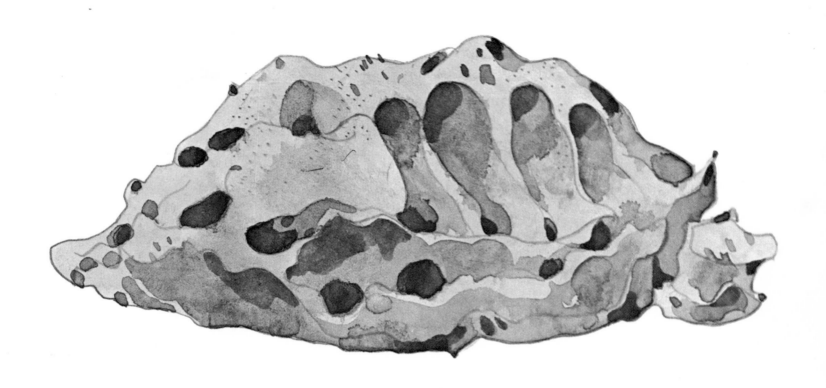

First I will play with the clay.

I will punch it and poke it and squeeze it
and roll it flat.

Jim has scissors and paper and glue.

Susan made a tower.

Olly put the puzzle

together.

Now I will make a road
in the pan of cornmeal.
I will drive the bulldozer.

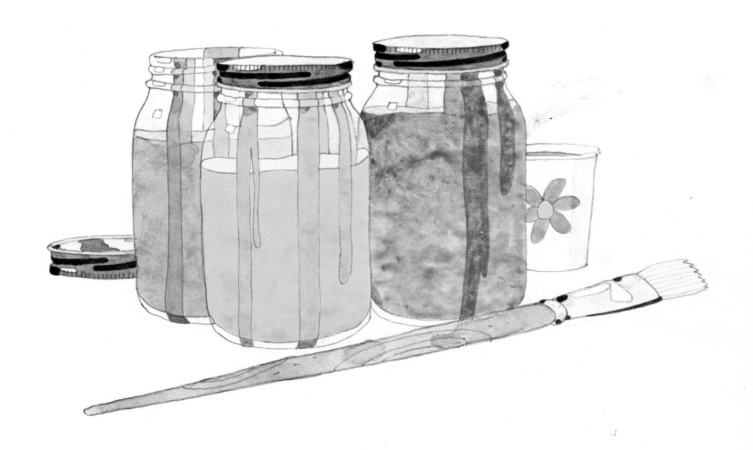

No, I think I will

paint a picture instead.

It is not raining,

so we can play outside.

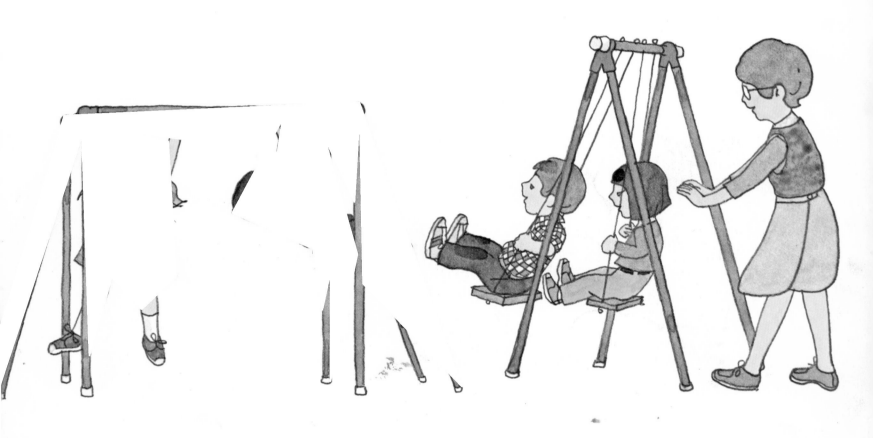

I can swing on the monkey bars.

But I am not a monkey!

We go inside to have
our juice and crackers. But Julia
doesn't want any juice today.

There is a bathroom with a sink

just high enough for me.

There are dolls and a carriage
and cars and trucks
and pots and pans and spoons.

This is the basket of dress-ups.

I like the shiny blue purse.

Lizzy likes the cowboy boots.

Paul likes the yellow hat.

I like this book because I like rabbits.

Mr. Doug is reading that one to Paul
and Susan and Olly.

We march and sing.

We bend and stretch.

Now it is time to go home.

But I will come again tomorrow.